BARNYARD BANTER

FOR LAURA GODWIN,
MY BANTERING BUDDY

Henry Holt and Company, LLC, *Publishers since 1866*
175 Fifth Avenue, New York, New York 10010
www.henryholt.com

Library of Congress Cataloging-in-Publication Data
Fleming, Denise.
Barnyard banter / Denise Fleming.
Summary: All the farm animals are where they should be, clucking
and mucking, mewing and cooing, except for the missing goose.
[1. Domestic animals—Fiction. 2. Animal sounds—Fiction.
3. Stories in rhyme.] I. Title.
PZ8.3.F6378Bar   1994   [E]—dc20   93-11032

First published in hardcover in 1994 by Henry Holt and Company
First paperback edition, 1997
Printed in the United States of America on acid-free paper. ∞

ISBN-13: 978-0-8050-1957-5 / ISBN-10: 0-8050-1957-X (hardcover)
15   14   13   12   11
ISBN-13: 978-0-8050-5581-8 / ISBN-10: 0-8050-5581-9 (paperback)
15   14   13

The illustrations for this book were created with handmade paper.

BARNYARD BANTER

Denise Fleming

Henry Holt and Company   New York

Cows in the pasture, moo, moo, moo

Roosters in the barnyard,

cock-a-doodle-doo

Hens in the henhouse,

cluck,

cluck,

cluck

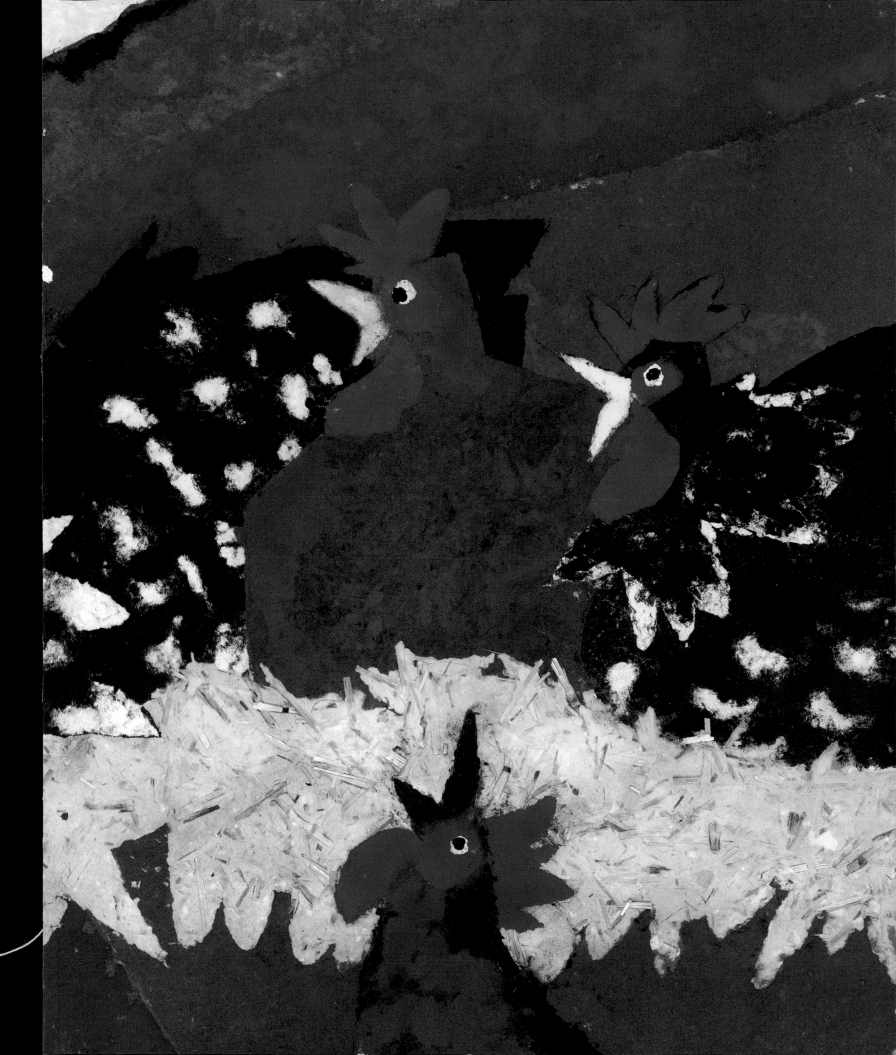

Pigs in the wallow,

muck,

muck,

muck

But where's Goose?

Kittens in the hayloft,

Pigeons
in the rafters,

COO, COO, COO

Donkeys in the paddock,

Crows
in the cornfield,

caw,

caw,

caw

**Crickets
in the stone wall,**

chirp,

chirp,

chirp

Frogs
in the farm pond,

burp, burp, burp

But where's Goose?

moo, moo, moo

cock -a- doodle -doo

cluck, cluck, cluck

muck, muck, muck

mew, mew, mew   coo, coo, coo

squeak, squeak, squeak

shriek, shriek, shriek

There's Goose!